This book belongs to:

. . . .

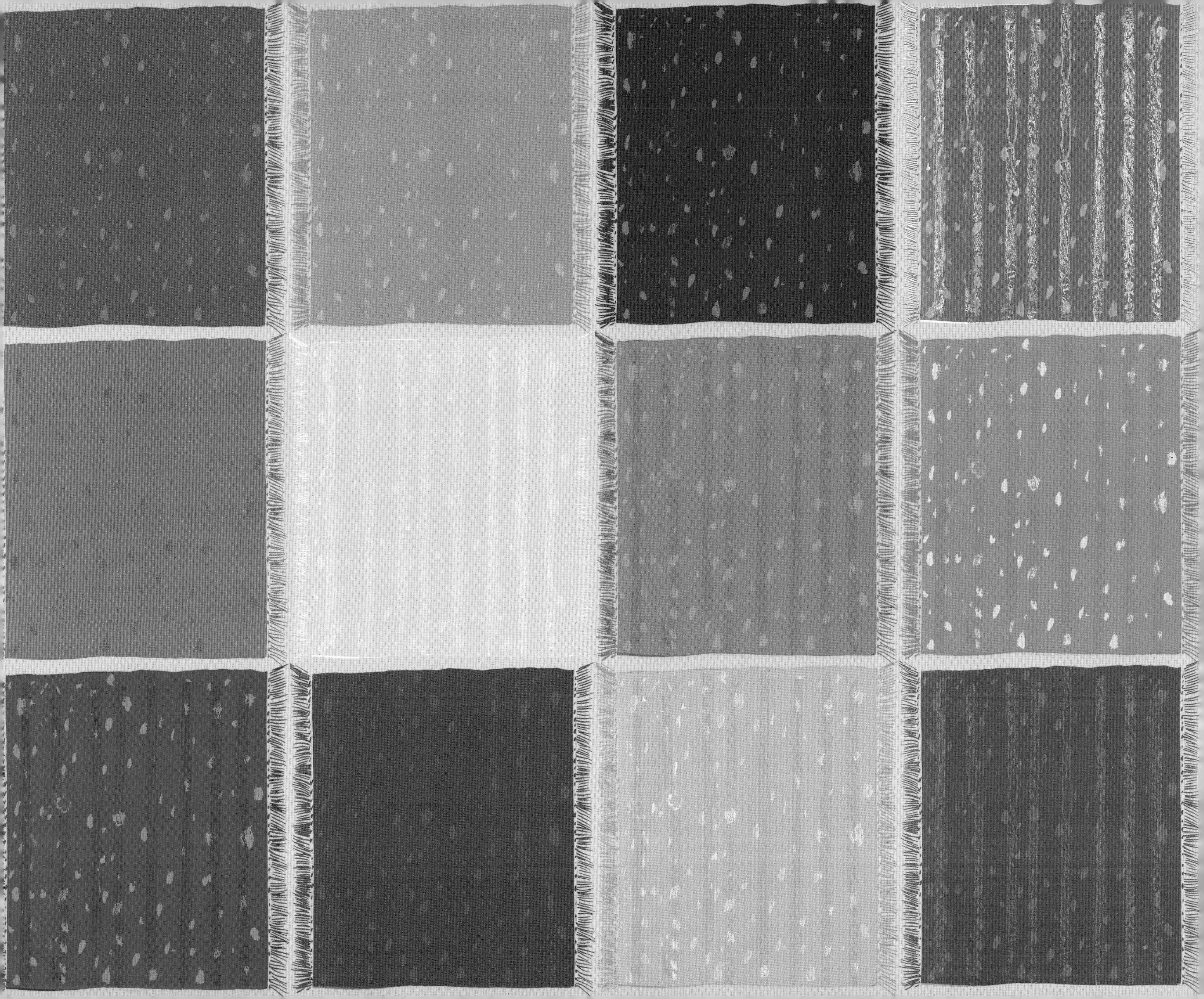

Great Clarendon Street, Oxford OX2 6DP

Oxford University Press is a department of the University of Oxford.
It furthers the University's objective of excellence in research, scholarship,
and education by publishing worldwide in

Oxford   New York

Auckland   Cape Town   Dar es Salaam   Hong Kong   Karachi
Kuala Lumpur   Madrid   Melbourne   Mexico City   Nairobi
New Delhi   Shanghai   Taipei   Toronto

With offices in

Argentina   Austria   Brazil   Chile   Czech Republic   France   Greece
Guatemala   Hungary   Italy   Japan   Poland   Portugal   Singapore
South Korea   Switzerland   Thailand   Turkey   Ukraine   Vietnam

Oxford is a registered trade mark of Oxford University Press
in the UK and in certain other countries

British Library Cataloguing in Publication Data available

ISBN: 978-0-19-278981-5 (paperback)

2 4 6 8 10 9 7 5 3 1

Printed in China

Paper used in the production of this book is a natural,
recyclable product made from wood grown in sustainable forests.
The manufacturing process conforms to the environmental
regulations of the country of origin

Brian Wildsmith's CAT ON THE MAT AND FRIENDS

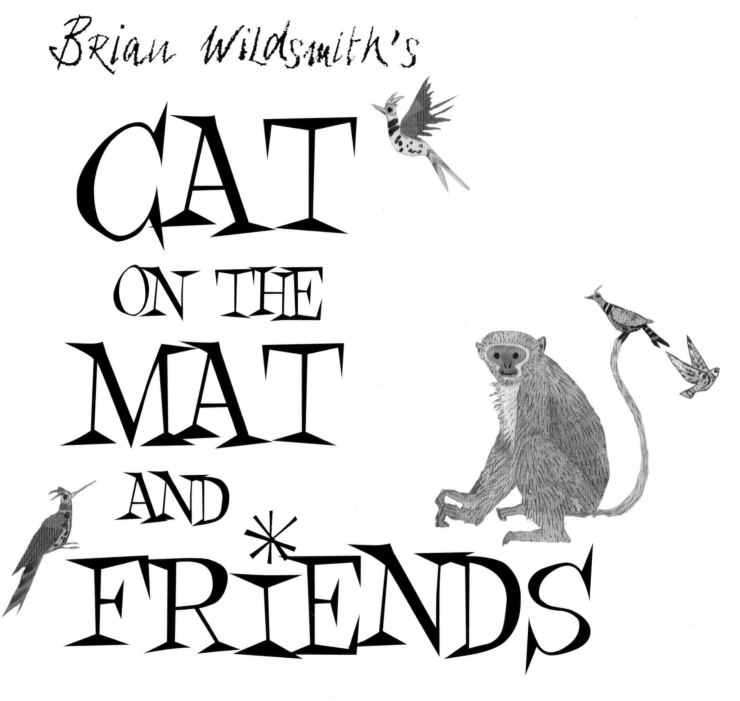

OXFORD

UNIVERSITY PRESS

CAT ON THE MAT

TOOT, TOOT

ALL FALL DOWN

THE ISLAND

CAT
ON
THE
MAT

The cat sat on the mat.

The dog sat on the mat.

The goat sat on the mat.

The cow sat on the mat.

The elephant sat on the mat.

'Sssppsst!'

The cat sat on the mat.

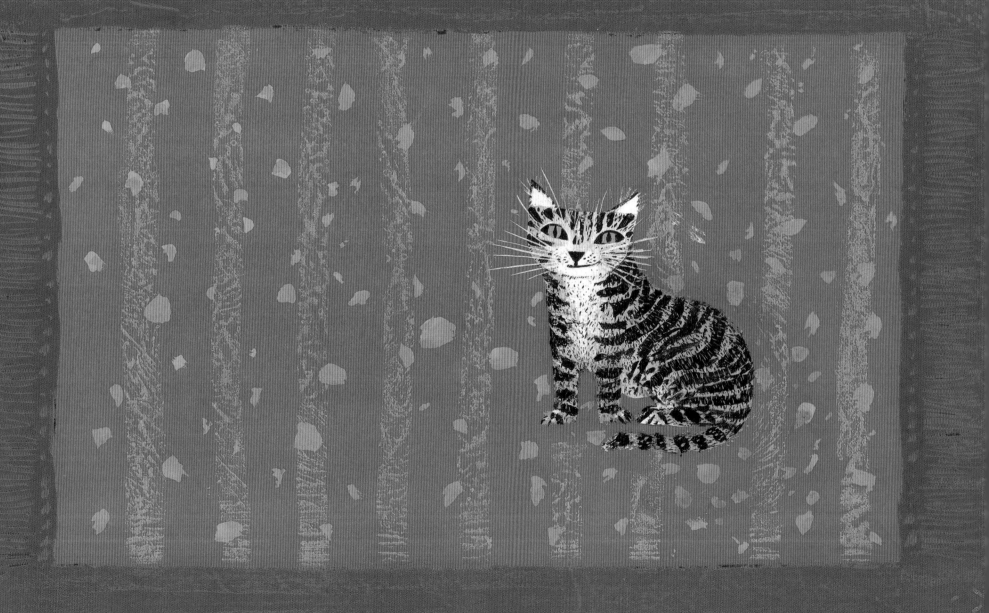

'Moo,' said the cow.

'Baa, baa,' said the sheep.

'Woof, woof, woof,' said the dogs.

'Miaow, miaow, miaow, miaow,'
said the cats.

'Cluck, cluck, cluck, cluck, cluck,' said the hens.

'Quack, quack, quack, quack, quack, quack,' said the ducks.

'Toot, toot,'
said the . . .

train!

And away they went.

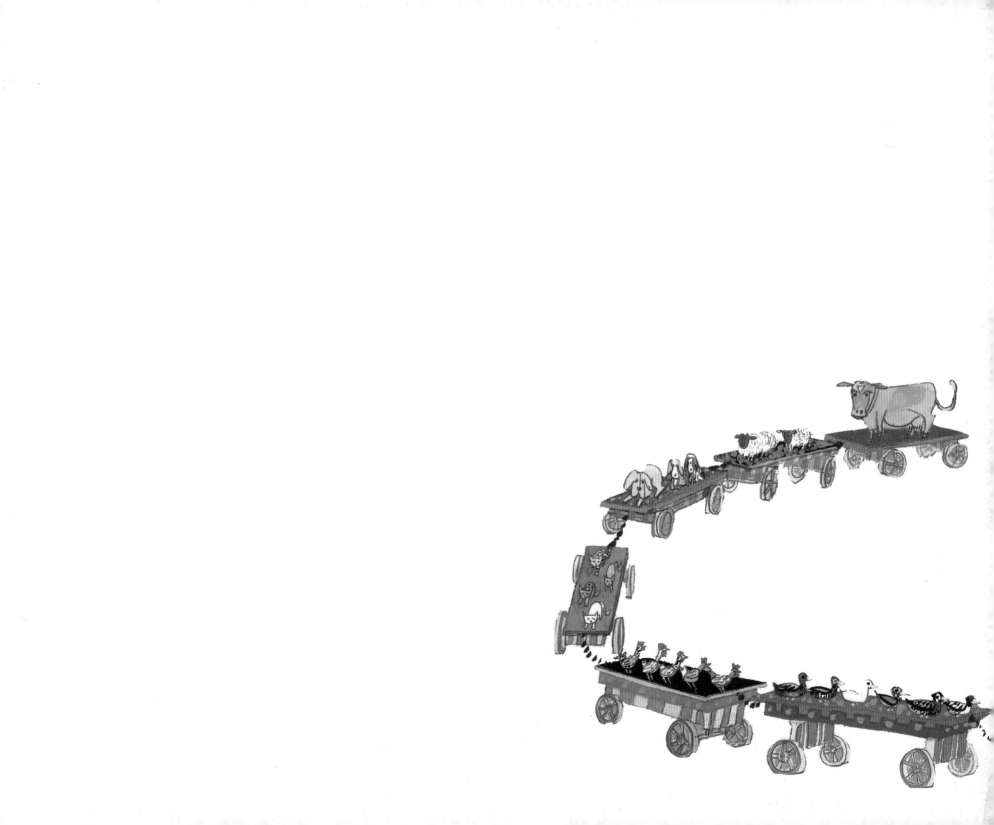

ALL
FALL
DOWN

I see a bee.

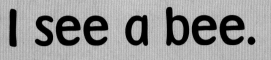

I see a bee
and a butterfly.

I see a bee and a butterfly and a bird.

I see a bee and a butterfly
and a bird and a rabbit.

I see a bee and a butterfly
and a bird and a rabbit
and a seal.

I see a bee

and a butterfly

and a bird

and a rabbit

and a seal

and a ball.

All fall

down!

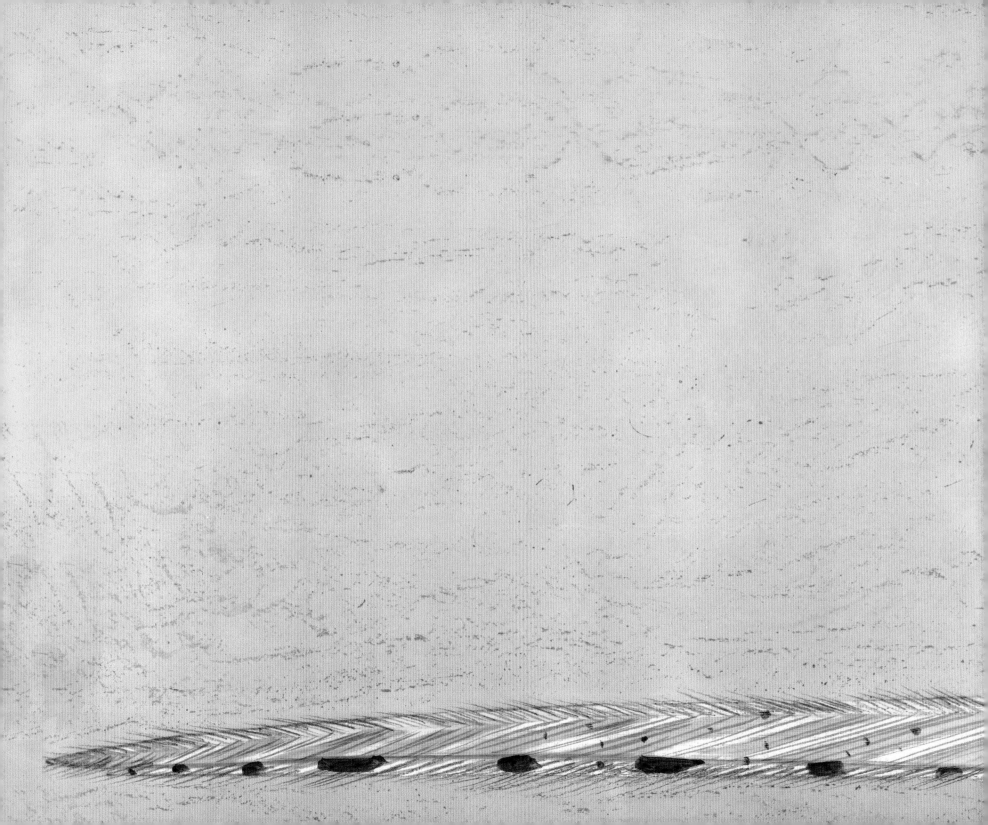

THE ISLAND

A leopard, goat, and monkey are on a raft.

'Look, there's an island!'

The leopard, goat, and monkey are on an island.

Down, down . . .

down they go.

'Hip, hip, hippooray!'

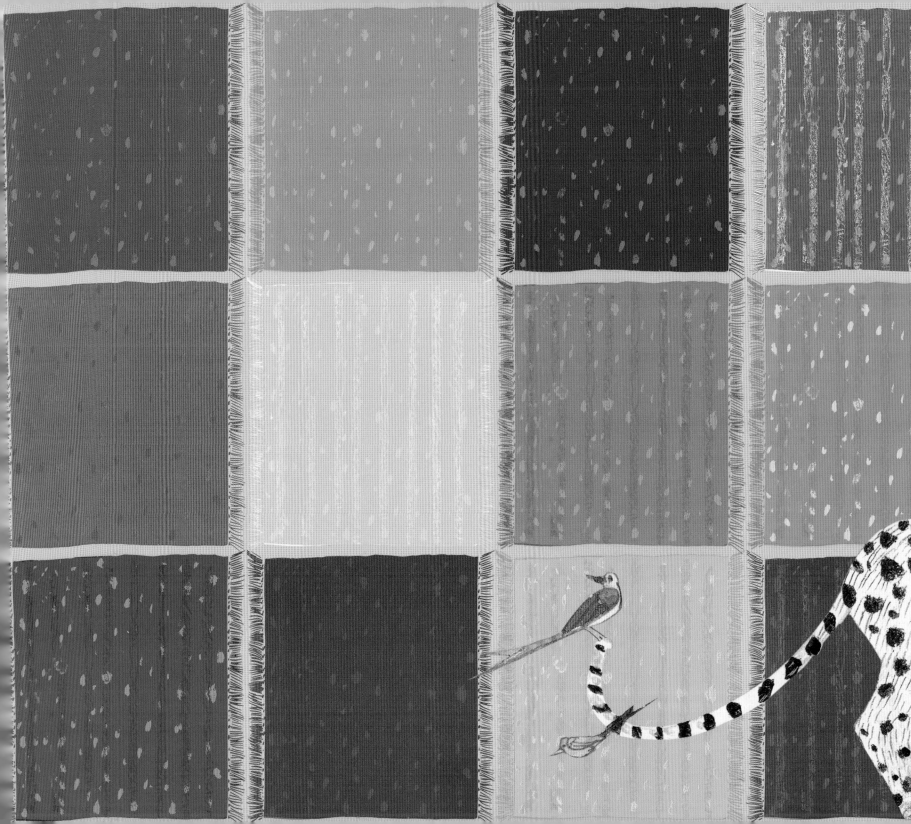

Toot, toot!